Boom! Rumble, rumble.

Did you hear that?

What was it?

 Uh-oh . . .

Yawn.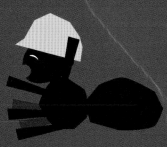

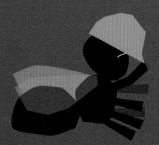 Huh?

It's an Orange
Aardvark!

Michael Hall

words & pictures

For Brady, Samantha, and Julianne

It's an Orange Aardvark!
Text and illustrations copyright © Michael Hall 2014

The right of Michael Hall to be identified as the Author and
Illustrator of this Work has been asserted by him in accordance
with the Copyright, Designs and Patent Act, 1988 (United Kingdom).

First published in the United States by Greenwillow Books,
an imprint of HarperCollins Children's Books, in 2014.
This edition first published in Great Britain in 2014 by
words & pictures, an imprint of Quarto Publishing Plc,
The Old Brewery, 6 Blundell Street, London N7 9BH
No part of this publication my be reproduced, stored in a retrieval system,
or transmitted in any form, or by any means, electrical, mechanical,
photocopying, recording or otherwise, without the prior written permission
of the publisher or a licence permitting restricted copying. In the United Kingdom
such licences are issued by the Copyright Licensing Agency, Saffron House,
6-10 Kirby Street, London EC1N 8TS.

A CIP catalogue record for this book is available from the British Library

ISBN 978-1-91027-704-1

1 3 5 7 9 8 6 4 2

Printed in China

Wrrrr . . .

What are you doing?

I'm making a hole in our stump
so we can see what's outside. *Wrrrr . . .*

Like a window!

Sweet!

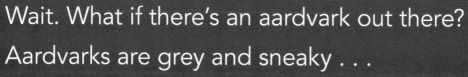

Wait. What if there's an aardvark out there?
Aardvarks are grey and sneaky . . .

and they have long tongues
that are perfect for eating carpenter ants,
you know!

Goodness! I'm scared.

Gracious! Me, too.

Yikes! Same here.

It's just a peephole.
Wrrrr . . .

THUNK!

It's not an aardvark.
It's orange!

Like an orange orange.

Juicy!

Oh no. It's an orange aardvark!

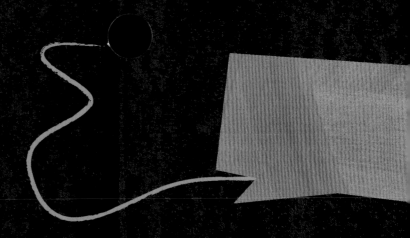

Aardvarks turn orange when they're
hungry for ants, you know.

Goodness!

Gracious!

Yikes!

Hold on,
I'll drill another hole
and we'll see.
Wrrrr . . .

THUNK!

Ah! It's orange and blue.

Blue like the ocean.

Cool!

Oh no, no!
It's worse than I thought.
It's an orange aardvark and . . .

it's wearing blue pyjamas!
Aardvarks love to snack on ants
before bed, you know.

Goodness!

Gracious!

Yikes!

Hold on. . . .
Wrrr . . .

THUNK!

Ah!
It's orange
and blue
and red!

Red like
a fire engine.

Awesome!

Oh no, no, no!
It's a pyjama-wearing
orange aardvark and . . .

it's carrying a large bottle of ketchup!
Aardvarks prefer their ants
with lots of ketchup, you know.

Goodness!

Gracious!

Yikes!

Hold on. I'll try again.
Wrrrr . . .

THUNK!

Ah!
It's orange, blue,
red, and green!

Green
like grass.

Neat!

Oh no, no, no, no!
It's a pyjama-wearing,
ketchup-carrying,
orange aardvark . . .

guiding a group of green geckos
to our stump!
Geckos eat ants, too,
you know.

Goodness!

Gracious!

Yikes!

Wrrr . . .

THUNK!

Look!
It's orange, blue, red,
green, and yellow!

Yellow like the sun.

Brilliant!

Oh no, no, no, no, no!
It's a pyjama-wearing,
ketchup-carrying,
gecko-guiding,
orange aardvark
and . . .

it's driving a yellow bulldozer
right toward our stump!

Goodness! I heard it rumbling.

Gracious! Me, too!

Yikes!

Hey, wait, you guys!

I just thought of something else
that's red, orange, yellow, green, and blue—
and it doesn't eat carpenter ants.
If I'm correct,
there should be purple
right about here.

Wrrrr . . .

THUNK!

Aha! It's purple!

Like a purple violet.

Let's go see!

Don't go!
It's a pyjama-wearing,
ketchup-carrying,
gecko-guiding,
dozer-driving,
orange aardvark
pouring purple
grape juice!

It's okay.
Come on out!

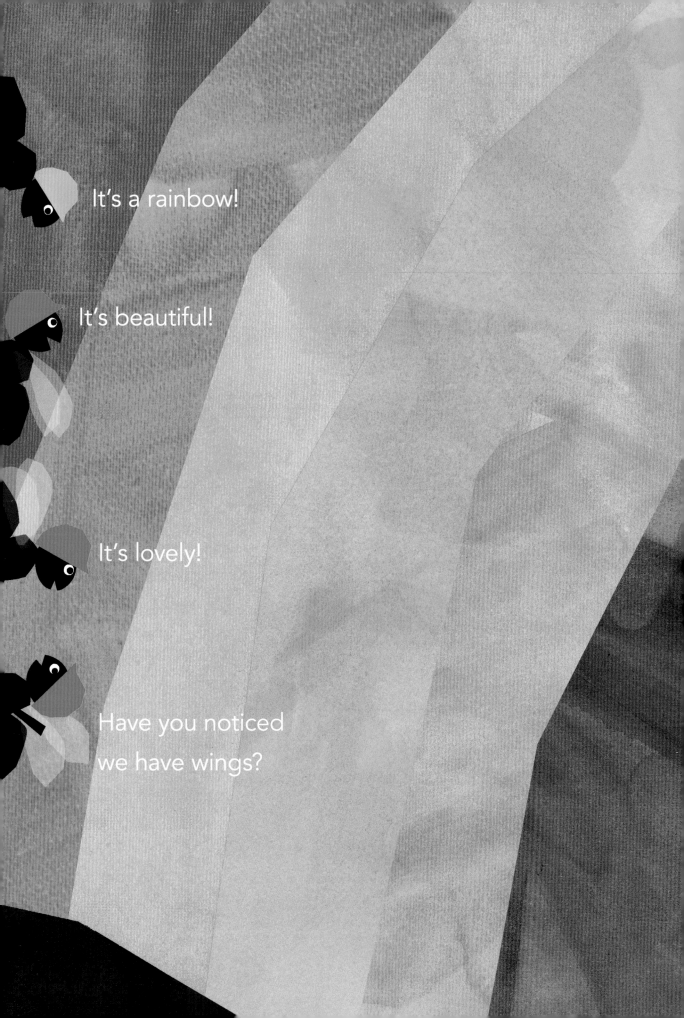

It's a rainbow!

It's beautiful!

It's lovely!

Have you noticed
we have wings?